Dear Reader,

The holiday season is a very special time of year, and all of us at the Reader Service would like to extend our warmest wishes to you and your loved ones.

We asked our editors to find us something really special as a Christmas gift for our Reader Service members and they have created this volume just for you!

It's our Christmas present to you, a small token of appreciation for being a loyal reader and for allowing us into your life... and into your heart!

We hope you enjoy this story, and we hope you have a Merry Christmas!

Season's greetings,
Pam Powers

MAURA SEGER

Starbright

Harlequin Books

HARLEQUIN BOOKS

All rights reserved, including the right to reproduce this book or portions thereof in any form whatsoever. For information address Harlequin Enterprises Limited, 225 Duncan Mill Road, Don Mills, Ontario, Canada M3B 3K9.

ISBN 0-373-15253-1

STARBRIGHT
Copyright © 1986 by Maura Seger
Originally published in Silhouette Christmas Stories
Copyright © 1986 by Silhouette Books

® are trademarks registered in the United States Patent and Trademark Office and in other countries.

Printed in U.S.A.

Chapter One

Who says you can't go home again? Mollie Williams was determined to do so. For days she had thought of nothing except getting out of Manhattan before Christmas, escaping the jam-packed streets, the brittle gaiety, the strained attempts at joviality that characterized the city during the holidays.

Not that she hadn't once seen it differently. There had been a time when she had thought New York the epitome of glamour, even of magic. Nothing, she had been sure, could ever come close to it. Not even the stars above could compete with the glitter of millions of lights, the aura of wealth and elegance, the pervasive sense of excitement and accomplishment.

When exactly her view had changed she didn't know, but change it had, and now to remain in the city an hour, a moment longer was intolerable. Not even the knowledge that she could spend the holidays with friends who were truly dear to her could make her linger. She wanted to be gone, far faster than the sluggish traffic and the stubborn lights would allow.

With an exclamation of mingled disgust and impatience she slumped behind the wheel of her BMW. That morning on the radio there had been a gridlock warning. Looking out at the impenetrable traffic along Fifth Avenue, she could see it had been warranted. Horns honked; drivers hollered; harried traffic cops tried to keep order. Pedestrians loaded down with packages swarmed around and between the stuck cars. When the light changed again it was impossible to move forward without running over a dozen oblivious people who went on their way with the insulated arrogance of true New Yorkers.

At last, after what seemed like hours, the cars lurched forward and she was able to turn onto a side street. It took Mollie "only" fifteen minutes to reach the next avenue. Within half an hour she had attained the F.D.R. Drive, which ran along the East River, and entered the stream of traffic heading north.

After that it wasn't too bad. Settling back in the seat, she turned on the radio, flipped past the stations playing Christmas carols and found herself some mellow music to while away the time. Vermont was, she estimated, eight hours away. If she drove straight through, she should be there in time for an early dinner.

Thoughts of the inn where she would be staying made her smile. There she would find peace and quiet, but even more importantly, she hoped to recapture a sense of the person she had once been, before life's often tumultuous, always unpredictable events engulfed her.

It didn't seem possible that she had turned thirty a few weeks before. As she had said to Joanna Wilkes, her neighbor and friend, "Last time I checked, I was twenty-three. What happened?"

The years had sped by so quickly. What she had once thought of as a substantial block of time had turned out to be as ephemeral as the glowing colors of a sunrise or a radiant autumn, difficult to hold even in memory. She could list the accomplishments of those years, and the defeats, but she had no real sense of where they had gone. And that troubled her, especially when she looked ahead and saw only more of the same.

Which was a good reason not to dwell on the future. For the first time in far too long she was actually taking a vacation, away from the ringing telephone, the constant meetings, the nonstop crises that typically plagued a new and rapidly growing business. She was getting away, feeling as guilty as a schoolchild playing hooky and at least as delighted. Never mind if it was only for a few days, she was going where she wanted to be.

"Williamstown, Vermont?" Joanna had said when Mollie told her of her plans. "Never heard of it."

"Neither have most people. It's a small town, actually a village, serving a farming community."

"Oh . . . that sounds very . . . nice." Trust Joanna to feel that way. The tall, willowy blonde left New York only for Paris, London and other cities of that ilk, or—if she really wanted to commune with nature—an exclusive Caribbean resort. Otherwise she claimed that being further than walking distance from Saks gave her a rash.

"You don't have to be polite about it," Mollie had assured her. "Lots of people would never give Williamstown a second look, but I love it, and I've been wanting to go back for quite a while."

Joanna had accepted that with a gesture conveying her abiding tolerance for human foibles. She had wished Mollie a good trip and gone back to buffing her nails. Joanna was a former model and newly minted actress with a role on a popular soap. The endless plot complications fascinated Mollie, who taped the show every day while she was at work and usually caught up in an orgy of watching on a weekend afternoon. Joanna's character was currently involved with daytime TV's latest heart-throb, Derek Eberhard, who played a ruthless, virile, and irresistible tycoon. The interaction between them was an unabashed mixture of sex and romance.

Remembering some of the more recent scenes—the ones that had threatened to send steam out of the TV set—Mollie sighed. She hated to admit it, but lately the lack of anything remotely similar in her own life had begun to trouble her.

Her hands tightened on the steering wheel. After Padraic, she had absolutely sworn that she was through with men. Better to be alone the rest of her life than to have to put up with the craziness, the arrogance, the sheer bullheadedness of the male of the species. Any woman with her head on straight knew they were only good for one thing, and Mollie could live well enough without that, thank you very much.

Or at least she had thought she could. What she was beginning to discover was that while life without sex wasn't so bad—not great, but not terrible, either—life without love was barren.

A red MG darted in front of her. She slammed on the brakes, blared the horn and shot the offending driver an angry look, all without interrupting her train of thought.

Had Padraic ever really loved her? Her full mouth tightened as remembered pain darkened her sapphire-blue eyes. What difference did it make, anyway? If what she had received from her ex-

husband had been love, then that emotion was sin-
gularly overrated.

The proof was to be found in how well she had
done since their separation and subsequent divorce. Only when she was free of him had she been
able to fulfill her own dreams, to find within herself the strength to build a highly successful fashion company turning out a line of clothes that
women across the country adored.

A Mollie Williams original—or, better yet, several of them—was the foundation of every savvy
woman's wardrobe. Her elegant, feminine, versa-
tile creations showed up in corporate boardrooms
and luxurious restaurants, but they were also immensely popular with women who had to scrimp to
afford them but thought the sacrifice well worthwhile. Very simply, Mollie knew that her clothes
made women feel *more*—more beautiful, more so-
phisticated, more confident, more at ease wher-
ever they went and whatever they did. That gave her
an immense sense of satisfaction, enough so that
until lately she had truly believed she had everything she wanted.

She sighed again and, as traffic narrowed to a
single lane that moved at a crawl, tilted her head
back against the seat. She'd meant to get a haircut
before leaving town, but there had been no time.
Her mane of wild cinnamon-hued waves billowed

out over her shoulders. "The soul of you," Padraic had called it, "trying to escape."

He was always saying things like that—dramatic, evocative, thrilling. But then, words were his business, and he knew how to use them. Or at least he had. She had no idea what he was doing these days and, she told herself, she didn't care. Geniuses like Padraic commonly burned themselves out early; if that had been his fate, she'd just as soon not know the details.

Past the outer edge of the city traffic at last smoothed out and she was able to pick up speed. It had snowed the previous day, a dusting that etched the barren trees and softened the frozen ground. Mollie remembered the white Christmases of her childhood and smiled wistfully. How kind Grania and Da had been. Both in their sixties when she had come to live with them, they nonetheless received her with all the devotion any child could want. The tragic death of their only child, Mollie's mother, in the same car accident that killed her husband was a blow from which they never fully recovered. But that did not prevent them from giving Mollie a home filled with love and laughter.

How she missed them. Grania's death some eight years before had been hard enough to bear, but when Da followed scant months later it had been almost more than she could stand. Looking back, she realized that she had still been numb with grief when she met Padraic. The passion they found together had, in a very real sense, brought her back to life. Perhaps that accounted for the extraordinary intensity of their relationship, which had progressed from first meeting to marriage in no more than a few weeks.

Her friends had thought it all wildly romantic. Padraic had already been a figure of near legendary proportions within the theater world, and well known beyond it. "The mad Irishman," he was called, not inaccurately. Directors, theater owners, backers, all threw up their hands in despair when they had to deal with him. Yet they were always willing enough to come back for more. Actors and actresses adored him, knowing as they did that each character that sprang from his incredible imagination was as rich a part as they would ever get.

He had been immensely talented beyond the understanding of most people, and to add to all his other gifts, he had even possessed the discipline needed to transform potential into actuality. Mollie had admired all that unstintingly, but she thought she could be forgiven for also sometimes wishing that he could be just a bit more human, more tolerant of her needs, more willing to put her ahead of his work some of the time.

As it was, she had always known exactly where she fitted into Padraic's life—in bed. They had never had any problems there, despite the fact that she had been a virgin when they met and shy about matching his passion with her own. For a while the pleasure they found together had been enough. Then it hadn't. She still didn't know when the transition had occurred, or why. All she was sure of was that she could never go back to the way she had been.

Not that she would ever have the opportunity. Men like Padraic Delaney were few and far between, all the more so since he had dropped out of sight.

Halfway to her destination Mollie pulled over at a gas station, stretched her limbs, bought a Coke and made a call to the office. Her assistant, Billy Barnes, twenty-four going on fifty, told her in no uncertain terms that everything was fine and she needn't given them another thought.

"We're peachy here," he said blithely. "The new Bombay silk is in and looks yummy. You're going to love it. Jennifer's talking to Wilbur again, so peace reigns in the cutting room. And they've added croissants to the coffee wagon."

"Sounds like I should go away more often."

"Well, of course we all miss you," Billy assured her. "But you need a break, so just relax and enjoy yourself. Oh, and Merry Christmas."

Mollie muttered her thanks, hung up, finished the Coke and tossed the can over her shoulder into the trash. She grinned at the appreciative whistle of the mechanic and got back in the car. Moments later she was on the road again, heading north.

Wasn't it great that everything was okay at the office? In fact, better than okay, considering how long Billy had been griping about the stale Danish and yucky donuts on the coffee wagon. Now he would have to find something else to complain about. Which wasn't fair, not even as a passing thought. He was a perfectly nice, hardworking, intelligent person whom she was lucky to have as an employee. Just as she was fortunate to have found all the people who worked for her. They were a great team, and she knew perfectly well they were responsible in large measure for her success. None of which explained why she was ticked off that they could get along without her.

Must be separation anxiety, she thought. This was the first time she had been away from the office for more than a couple of days since starting the company. At first she had slept on a cot beside her desk, working seven days a week, eighteen hours a day. Lately it hadn't been anywhere near that bad, but she still felt funny taking a whole week off.

Still insecure, Williams. Still not quite able to accept your success and believe it will last. Padraic had warned her about that, during their last huge fight. He'd said her biggest problem was a lack of faith in herself. He'd accused her of looking to him to provide her with a sense of identity and purpose, and made it quite clear that he had no intention of doing so. She'd hurled back her own set of charges—that he was insensitive, egotistical and uncaring. That he thought of nothing except his writing and sex. That he expected her to be there when he wanted the latter, and to be invisible the rest of the time. Most of all, she had hurled angry words at him about Jessica. Words he had not bothered to refute.

So that had been that. She'd gone on her own, founded Mollie Williams Fashions, worked like a Trojan to make it a success, and was now basking in the glory of her own accomplishments. Supposedly. Maybe going home would help her work that out.

Home. Such a lovely word. Barely had she reached the outskirts of Williamstown, the settlement founded by her ancestors some two hundred years before, than she began to recapture the wonderful sense of belonging she had once known there.

But then why wouldn't she, when Williamses had lived in the village in an unbroken line stretching back to the original founders? She was the last of them, and it wasn't until she had left that there were no more Williamses in Williamstown.

Leaving had been almost the toughest thing she had ever done. Only her parting from Padraic had cost her more. But she'd had no choice, not when she needed every penny she could get her hands on to start her business. The old farmhouse she'd inherited from her grandparents had been her only tangible asset.

During the divorce proceedings Padraic had suggested that he'd be willing to put up the money to help her get started. Mollie truly believed she would have died before accepting it. As it was she'd had barely enough to rent dingy office space and buy materials. But that was all behind her now, and she wasn't going to dwell on it. Not when she was finally beginning to feel really excited about being back.

It seemed that nothing had changed in the village. Main Street was still lined with Colonial-style buildings, many of which dated from the previous century, while the rest looked as if they did. The maple trees planted decades before at regular intervals along the street were decorated with small, twinkling lights. Pine wreaths hung on every door, their scent filling the air.

It was snowing lightly, soft flakes dancing past her windshield. She turned a corner, then another, and came at last to the Rooster Inn, a rambling roadside stopping place added onto over many generations and set on a slight rise overlooking the rest of the village. Mollie parked the car, got out, and stood for a moment looking at the comfortable old building. It was so well remembered from her childhood that she could hardly believe that it, too, hadn't changed. But then, she supposed that Jeremiah Withers, who had inherited the inn a few years before, took great pride in keeping it in top condition.

Gathering her mink coat more closely around her—it had been her thirtieth birthday present to herself—she walked up the flagstone path. In her hand was a Gucci suitcase holding the essentials she expected to need during the next week. Bells jangled as she opened the door and stepped inside.

Mollie stopped in the hall and looked around appreciatively. All her senses were alert to the pleasures surrounding her. Collector's pieces of Early American and Shaker furniture glowed in the late-afternoon sunlight, the rich patina of their woods turned to burnished gold and copper. The mingled scents of a wood fire and baking bread settled over her like a feather-light blanket of down. She could hear a piano being played nearby and a handful of voices, untrained but charming, raised in song.

Eagerly she moved on to the room from which the music came. A dozen or so people were there, most gathered around the piano, the rest seated at the long wooden bar or at the tables scattered around the room. Over the large fireplace stretched a magnificent pair of elk's antlers topped with

Christmas wreaths. Behind the bar, wiping it down with a white cloth, was Jeremiah Withers.

Mollie approached him with a broad smile. "Jerry, it's good to see you again. You haven't changed at all." That was true. He was still the same tall, lanky man with the shy eyes and the gentle manner that she remembered. What did surprise her was the sudden blush that spread across his cheeks when he saw her.

"Mollie...it's you...." he said, the cloth abruptly halting in midair.

"Why...yes, it is. You sound so surprised. Have I changed that much?" It had been five years since she'd last been in Williamstown, and a great deal had happened in that time, but surely not enough to justify his reaction. He seemed almost embarrassed, which made no sense at all.

"No," he said, hastily folding the cloth and tucking it under the bar. "That is, you look great."

"Thanks," she said dryly, aware that they had become the objects of interest of the other people in the bar, who were looking at them curiously. "You did get my letter?"

"Letter?"

"About the room." He must have received it; she had a confirmation of her reservation in her pocketbook.

"Oh... that. Oh... listen, Mollie, I'm awfully sorry about this, but there's a problem. I guess maybe I should have called you."

"Problem?" Her voice had dropped, becoming tight. The last thing she wanted to deal with was a problem of any sort, certainly not one that involved her long-awaited vacation.

"Yes... you see, we have some other people staying here, and they were supposed to check out, only they haven't, and I can't very well... that is, I could ask them to leave, but it doesn't seem right. Not with Christmas and all. You know, just to throw them out on the street."

"All right, I'll take another room."

"That's just it." He glanced away abashedly. "There aren't any."

"I don't understand...." He couldn't be serious. She hadn't come so far, all the way home, to be turned back now.

"I'm sorry," Jeremiah said gently. "But all our rooms are filled. There's no place for you to stay here."

"But..." She shook her head disbelievingly. Jeremiah had been her friend; surely he must have some idea of what coming back meant to her. How could he simply turn her away? "Maybe... there's someplace else. Another inn?"

"I'm afraid not. The Rooster's still the only one in town."

He didn't even look particularly sorry about that. In fact, he'd returned to wiping the bar, as though expecting her to simply leave.

Instead Mollie drew herself up to her full five feet eight inches and faced him squarely. "Now look here, Jeremiah, I won't be treated like this. I've had a long trip, I'm tired, and I want a room. It's all very well for you to say that—"

"There's nothing I can do," he insisted.

"There has to be."

"'Fraid not. Of course, you might be able to find a room in somebody's house, though I expect most people are full up already with relatives and friends."

"I don't want to stay with strangers."

"Then stay with me."

At the sound of the deep, smooth voice coming from behind her, Mollie whirled around. Her eyes widened in disbelief. She couldn't possibly be seeing what she seemed to be....

Padraic Delaney looked back at her imperturbably, a sardonic smile curving his lean mouth and an unholy light burning in his emerald eyes.

Chapter Two

"What are you doing here?" Mollie demanded, only half expecting the apparition before her to reply. Padraic couldn't possibly have just walked back into her life as though he had never left it, offering her a place to stay and acting as though there was nothing at all untoward about his sudden reappearance.

"Having a drink," he said. "Care to join me?" Before she could respond, other than to open her mouth and stare, he signaled to Jeremiah. "Two brandies, please, Jerry. We'll have them by the fire."

"We will not," Mollie said, finally regaining her voice. "You do what you want, but I'm leaving."

"And going where?" He spoke softly, but the rough timbre of his voice vibrated clear through her. As it always had, especially at night when they'd lain in bed together after making love, speaking softly of the things lovers talk about.

Stop that! She was crazy to be indulging in such memories, especially now, when the man who starred in them was standing right in front of her.

He really was there, she realized with a deadening sense of inevitability. It wasn't her imagination playing crazy tricks on her.

There were the same broad shoulders and powerful chest, the narrow waist and lean hips that she remembered so well. His hair was still thick and black, though faintly touched by silver now. His broad, craggy face—too powerful to be called handsome—hadn't changed, except perhaps to acquire a few more character lines that only added to his appeal. His green eyes, deeply set and thickly lashed, were still riveting. And his slanted brows remained a barometer of his mood, expressing both challenge and skepticism, as though daring her to walk out the door and prove to him that she didn't have the courage to spend even a few minutes in his company.

"All right," she snapped. "I'll have a drink, but that's all. Then I have to find someplace to stay." There were several motels outside of town; she'd spend the night at one of them and head back to New York the next morning. Hardly the way she had imagined spending the holidays, but that was just too bad. Obviously fate had never intended her to return, so the sooner she left the better.

"You already have a place," Padraic said as he took her elbow and steered her toward the fire. The touch of his hand, even through the layers of her fur coat and the soft wool dress she wore beneath, was electrifying. She jerked away as though stung and glared at him.

"You can't be serious. There's no way I'd share your room." She presumed he was staying at the inn, though she couldn't imagine why. The few times she had managed to get him up to Williamstown he had been thoroughly bored and anxious to return to the city.

"You don't have to," he said as he took the two snifters of brandy from Jeremiah and set them on a low table near the fire. "It's a good-sized house I have, with plenty of room for you."

Dimly Mollie remembered that whenever he was particularly anxious about something he had a tendency to slip back into the speech rhythms of his Dublin childhood. That he had just done so puzzled her, though she didn't care to dwell on it. Other matters were more pressing.

"A house? You mean you're actually living here?" Padraic? The man who claimed there was no civilization outside the city and that being exposed to large chunks of sky undivided by buildings made him dizzy?

"A man's entitled to change, wouldn't you say?" he inquired. "I've decided I like the country. It's very...inspiring."

Gingerly Mollie sat down across from him and reached for her brandy. She took a sip, eyeing him over the rim of the glass. "You're writing again?"

He frowned slightly. "What makes you think I ever stopped? Heavens, woman, you ought to remember writing's like breathing to me."

"I thought it was," she agreed, "but there's been nothing from you in so long." Padraic's last play, *Winners and Losers*, had premiered shortly after their divorce to critical acclaim and a slew of prizes. It was still running three years later, a feat almost unheard of for a nonmusical. But since then there had been only silence.

"That doesn't mean I'm not working," he assured her. Leaning back in the chair, his big body apparently at ease, he looked perfectly at home in an environment where he had once been anything but. The blue chambray shirt stretched over his broad chest, the khaki trousers covering his long legs and the tweed jacket hung over the back of the chair were all well made but casual. He sat with one leg crossed over the other, a foot resting on the opposite knee, giving her a view of worn work boots with a few clumps of dirt clinging to the cleated soles.

Looking at him more closely Mollie saw that he was lightly tanned, and that the skin over his high cheekbones was ruddy, as though frequently exposed to sun and wind. His large hands, with their long, blunt-tipped fingers, were slightly chapped and, when he reached for his glass, she saw calluses on his palms.

"What have you been doing?" she asked. "Besides writing."

"This and that. You know what it's like living in the country; there's always something that needs seeing to."

True enough, except that she had a hard time picturing Padraic chopping wood, repairing a stone wall, milking a cow, or doing anything else of the sort. His idea of exercise had always been either a long, solitary run in the park or a savagely paced game of racquetball.

"Enough about me," he said. "I hear your company is a great success. Congratulations."

"Thanks," Mollie replied, a bit unsteadily. She was surprised, not to say disconcerted, that he knew anything at all about what she had been doing. Not only that, but he seemed genuinely happy for her, which severely diminished any chance she might have had to say "I told you so." Not, of course, that she would have indulged in anything so childish. It was only that she might have enjoyed pointing out to him how well she had done on her own.

Padraic watched the play of emotion across her face and repressed a smile. After the first shock of actually seeing her again he had settled down enough to drink in the sight of her. She was even more beautiful than he remembered. There was a piquancy about her delicate features that never failed to take his breath away.

Her unusually large blue eyes had always dominated her face, not only because of their size and loveliness, but because of the soul that shone through them. When she was happy they sparkled with silver lights. When she was sad or upset, as he sensed she was now, the glow was dimmer, as though a veil had fallen between her and the rest of the world.

The first time he had seen her, she had made him think of a forest sprite wary of being caught by the eye of man, let alone touched by him. Back then, when she was twenty-two and he was thirty, she had been all coltish angles and half-formed curves, the promise of a woman not yet fulfilled.

Now that was changed. From the top of her wild hair, in which the glowing whisper of the fire was caught, to the bottom of her slender feet, shod in the softest of leather pumps, she was a remarkably lovely thing. She had removed her coat when they sat down, revealing an elegantly draped dress of sapphire wool, one of her own designs, he guessed. It lightly skimmed her tall, slender body, managing at once to be both utterly proper and devastatingly sensual—not unlike the woman herself.

Padraic swallowed a large portion of his brandy and bade the memories stay away. He'd had enough of them over the long years. To be confronted with them again at the same time that he was looking at the cause would be too much.

"It's a remarkable coincidence," Mollie said slowly. "Our both turning up here at the same time."

Padraic shrugged. "These things happen. Besides, if you think about it, it really isn't all that remarkable. After all, I live here and you used to, so why shouldn't we run into each other?"

She didn't have an answer to that. Surely he must be right. The alternative, that the meeting had somehow been arranged, was ridiculous. Had Padraic needed to get in touch with her, he could have done so easily enough through her lawyer. Not that she could think why he would want to. Whatever they had once shared was long since over and done with.

Uneasy at his steady scrutiny, she glanced out the window. "It's starting to get dark. I'd better be going." Despite herself, the reluctance she felt as she contemplated the ruin of her plans was evident.

"Forget about finding a motel," Padraic urged. "You'll be more comfortable staying with me."

His weren't the only eloquent eyebrows; hers bespoke skepticism fluently. "I doubt that very much."

"Why? Surely we're long past the stage when we couldn't be pleasant to each other. You need a room, I have a spare, so why shouldn't you use it?"

"It's not that simple."

"It is if we want it to be," he insisted.

Mollie was tempted. The chance to spend a little time with Padraic was all but irresistible. That worried her. She fervently wished that she could feel nothing for him, but watching the play of light and shadow across his rugged features, she knew that wasn't the case.

Once she had loved him with all her heart and soul. Then, for a brief time, she had truly hated him. After that there had been only numbness, which now seemed to be fading with dangerous swiftness as pinpricks of awareness and need darted through her. She shifted uneasily in her chair and looked at him closely.

"Why are you being so nice to me?"

He lifted his eyes to heaven. "What a question to ask. Aren't you used to people being nice?"

"Sometimes . . . but not you. You're wonderful or you're terrible, never anything in-between."

He was silent for a long moment before he said, "I suppose I do tend toward extremes."

He sounded so regretful that Mollie couldn't stop herself from reaching out to him. Her hand touched his lightly. "That's just the way you are. There's no reason to wish otherwise."

"No?" His fingers curled around hers, warm and strong. "I could think of several reasons, but never mind. Shall we get started?"

"You're presuming I'll come with you."

He shook his head. "I'm presuming you're too kindhearted not to accept my offer in the spirit in which it's given."

"And that is?" she asked.

"Friendship, nothing more. Perhaps we won't be able to manage it, but I'd at least like to try."

While she thought it over he settled up with Jeremiah, who was doing his best not to look at either of them. The innkeeper murmured something Mollie didn't quite catch. She was too preoccupied, trying to come to terms with the idea of being friends with Padraic. They had never been that. Lovers, yes, sometimes adversaries, but never friends. There had always been far too much passion between them to allow for calm affection.

Yet it might still be possible. Time was, after all, supposed to heal all hurts. After three years it was important to her to believe that she could take Padraic in stride.

"All right," she said suddenly. "I'll stay with you, but only for tonight. Tomorrow I'm heading back to the city."

"Why?" he asked as they left the inn. It had begun to snow more heavily. Fat flakes drifted past them in the gathering twilight. An inch or so had already accumulated on the ground. Instinctively Mollie accepted Padraic's arm to keep herself from slipping.

"Surely there's no reason for you to rush back," he said as they reached her car. "Hadn't you planned to spend Christmas here?"

"At the inn. Since that isn't possible I may as well go back and get some work done."

His brows drew together in a dark scowl, and for a moment she thought she was about to witness an eruption of the famous Delaney temper. That faded as quickly as it had come, and he smiled mildly. "Why don't we talk about that in the morning?" Before she could answer he held open the car door for her, helped her in and closed it carefully. "I'm driving a red pickup," he said. "You shouldn't have any trouble following."

Mollie didn't, at least not at first. It wasn't until they turned off onto a dirt road running deep into the forest that she began to think there had been some mistake. The route they were following was all too familiar to her, though she had thought never to take it again. That she might had briefly occurred to her when she was planning her trip, but she had deliberately put the idea out of her mind.

It was one thing to return to her hometown for a few days; it was quite another to deliberately subject herself to all the memories, and all the regrets, that would come if she ever again set foot in the beloved farmhouse that had been her grandparents, and that she had been forced to sell in order to realize her dreams.

Yet it now appeared that was exactly what she was expected to do. Mollie's throat grew tight again and her heart pounded painfully when she drew up behind the red truck parked in front of the two-story house set in a clearing surrounded by ancient oak and maple trees. A stream ran nearby, and off to one side she could see the old stone well, long since boarded over. On either side of the porch rhododendron bushes had their leaves folded against the cold. The lawn was covered with snow on which she could see the tracks of a few late-foraging birds and squirrels.

Padraic had gotten out of the truck. Hastily, before he could get too close, she slipped from the car and stood staring at the house. For all her absorption, she was well aware of him when he came to her side.

"How long..." Her voice sounded like sandpaper on old wood. She stopped, cleared her throat, and tried again. "How long have you been renting it?" Please let it only be for a week or two; please let him be quickly on his way back out of her life.

"I haven't. I bought the house when you put it on the market three years ago."

Mollie turned and faced him squarely. "Why?"

He shrugged and let his gaze fall away. "Why not?" At her sharp intake of breath, signaling as he well knew the end of her patience, he went on quickly. "I'd decided to get out of the city, and I needed a place to live. Williamstown was the only small town I knew of, so it was only natural to start looking here. When the real estate agent told me the farmhouse was on the market I grabbed it.''

She tugged her coat more closely around her, trying to shut out a chill she knew came from deep inside. ''That doesn't make any sense. You hated the house. I was only able to get you to visit a couple of times, and you made it quite clear you didn't enjoy yourself.''

''Yes . . . I suppose I did.'' His eyes were hooded as he jerked his head toward the porch. ''The snow's getting heavier, and it's cold. Let's go inside.''

Mollie didn't want to. Every instinct for survival that she possessed told her to get back into her car and put as much distance as she possibly could between herself and her ex-husband. He was altogether too compelling, and too dangerous. With very little effort he could make her forget all the staunch resolutions that guided her in her new life.

Except that she couldn't quite muster the strength to walk away, not from both Padraic and her grandparents' house. She might have been able to resist them separately, though she suspected that was debatable, but together they were too potent a reminder of her past to be ignored.

Besides, she was all but overwhelmed by curiosity to see what he had done to the place. With any luck he had ruined it, in which case she could leave with a clear conscience.

Luck, it seemed, wasn't with her. Barely had she stepped into her childhood home than she realized it had been receiving tender, loving care. Although much had changed—the walls were freshly painted; the floors and staircase had been sanded; the heavy, rather dour furniture she remembered was gone—much had also remained the same. Most importantly the sense of warmth and welcome she had always associated with the house was not only intact but stronger than ever.

She managed a shaky laugh. "I'm surprised."

"I realize it isn't exactly the same...."

"No, it isn't that. It's lovely. If I'd been able to keep the house I had all sorts of plans about what to do with it. Plans you seem to have carried out, yet..." She turned to him, her blue eyes filled with bewilderment. "I never told you about them, did I?"

He shook his head. "No, we never discussed that. Perhaps I just picked up some of your feelings for the old place."

She had never considered Padraic to be particularly sensitive to her feelings, let alone any so private as her love for the house he had disparaged. Yet there must be something to what he was saying, because he truly had captured her vision of what might have been.

How disconcerting to discover that what she had thought was locked forever in her mind existed quite firmly in reality. How disturbing to wonder what else she had long since come to think of as impossible might actually be within her grasp.

Chapter Three

"You look tired," Padraic said gently. "Why don't you go upstairs and get settled in while I see about dinner?"

Mollie nodded absently. She was still struggling to come to terms with being in the house. Climbing the stairs, she noted that they still creaked in all the same places. At the top she suddenly thought of something and turned around, surprised to find Padraic still standing in the hall looking up at her.

"How will I know which is the guest room?"

"It's your old room. I took your grandparents'."

Of course, she should have expected that. The only other room on the second floor, besides the bath, was a tiny cubicle under the eaves that Grania had used for sewing. Telling herself that it didn't matter, she walked down the short corridor and gingerly opened the door she knew so well. A sigh of relief escaped her as she realized that her former room, like the rest of the house, had been redecorated.

The narrow oak bed she had slept in was gone, as were the battered pine dresser she had used and the old school desk where she had done her homework. In their place was a delightful four-poster bed of shaker design covered with a traditional Lone Star pattern quilt in white and blue. A braided rag rug in the same colors covered the floor. White lace curtains hung at the windows. A golden pine armoire took up most of one wall, with a matching dresser opposite it. On the dresser a poinsettia plant in a wicker basket added a festive touch.

Much of the tension Mollie had been feeling ever since she walked into the inn and discovered her plans had gone awry began to ease. She unpacked quickly, placing her few toiletries on the dresser. The lacy underwear she favored and two equally feminine nightgowns went into a drawer. In the closet she hung the slacks, shirts and sweaters she had brought, along with the long black evening skirt she had added at the last minute. On the back of the door she hung her wooly white robe, chosen more for practicality than looks. She had expected the inn to be drafty, and while the house was less so, it too had its cold patches.

That done, she ran a brush through her hair in a futile effort to give it some sense of order. The gesture was made out of habit; no matter how many times she had tried to tame the riot of cinnamon waves she had never even come close to succeeding. Admitting defeat yet again, she left the brush on the dresser and went back downstairs.

Padraic was in the kitchen, standing in front of a six-burner stove that looked as though it belonged in a gourmet restaurant. He was stirring a large pot from which tempting aromas wafted.

She was about to comment on the incongruity of the situation, having never seen him so much as boil water before, when two things simultaneously captured her attention. One was the large, beautifully decorated Christmas tree in the far corner of the kitchen, near the fireplace. The other was the Irish wolfhound that had just hurled itself at her and was busy licking her face.

"O'Casey!" she exclaimed with delight, prompting his tail to wag all the more fiercely and his tongue to scrub all the more devotedly. They had been great pals, she and O'Casey, in the years she was with Padraic. The dog had been little more than a pup when she first met him and, though devoted to his master, he had wholeheartedly accepted her as the second most important person in his life. Apparently he hadn't forgotten.

"Down boy," Padraic said with gentle firmness. The dog obeyed instantly, but sat on his haunches scant inches from Mollie's feet, his eyes on her adoringly and his tongue lolling at the ready.

"I've missed O'Casey," she said as she scratched the dog behind his ear.

"At least that's something."

"What?"

"Never mind. Dinner's almost ready. That is, if you still like bouillabaisse."

Mollie assured him that she did. The spicy seafood stew had always been one of her favorites. "Don't tell me you just whipped this up," she teased as, following his directions, she took French bread from the oven where it had been warming and sliced it.

"I made it this morning. It's better when it's had a chance to sit for a few hours."

"When did you learn to cook?"

"After I moved up here. It was that or starve." He smiled as he ladled two large bowls full of the stew. "You know how it is here, everyone's expected to be self-reliant."

"True, but you could have hired someone to come in to help."

"I preferred to be by myself for a while."

That was all he said, but Mollie got the feeling there had been a great deal more to his decision to isolate himself in the country than he was saying. Even if she had felt up to questioning him further, there was no opportunity as he neatly changed the subject.

"What do you think of the tree?"

"It's lovely, just like the ones I remember from..." She stopped and, at the quick flash of acknowledgment in his eyes, peered more closely at the decorations. Wooden soldiers in gaily painted uniforms, sparkling birds with golden beaks and shimmering glass ornaments danced in front of her eyes. On the top of the tree was a white dove. Nestled within the branches was a very old, fragile angel holding a lyre. "H-how...how did you get these?"

"They were in the attic," Padraic said as he set the bowls on the table. "You must have left them here after our last Christmas together."

She had done exactly that, and had managed not to think of them since. They were the decorations from her childhood, except for the dove, which she had purchased herself. How well she remembered that day. She and Padraic had had yet another fight, and she had gone off by herself so that he wouldn't see her tears or her pain.

Wandering through the streets, feeling sorry for herself because Christmas was coming even as she suspected her marriage was ending, she had spied the dove in a store window. Some impulse, perhaps lingering hopefulness, had driven her to buy it, and later to return to their apartment and persuade Padraic to come to Williamstown with her for the holiday.

He'd gone along despite the fact that the one other trip he'd made there had not been a success. Buoyed by her own enthusiasm, Mollie hadn't noticed the lack of his until it was too late. Only afterward did she realize that he had been in the throes of writing an extremely difficult play, one that he hadn't been sure he would ever be able to finish.

Genius was a harsh taskmaster. Padraic put more of himself into what he did than anyone she knew. Unfortunately, that had left very little for anything else, including their relationship.

Despite her best efforts the holiday had turned out to be tense and cheerless. Before it was over they had fought again and gone back to the city separately. One of the last things she had done before leaving was to pack up the Christmas ornaments and put them away in the attic.

"I'm surprised you bothered with a tree," she said as he held her chair for her and she slipped into it. "That sort of sentiment never seemed to appeal to you."

He took his place opposite her and reached for the wine to fill both their glasses. "I did manage to give you that impression, didn't I?"

"Are you saying it wasn't true?"

"No, only that it was incomplete." At her puzzled look he explained, "I never let you see why I didn't like holidays, all the excitement and the expectations. But then, there's so much I never let you even glimpse."

Mollie had always suspected as much, but she was astonished to hear him admit it. Early on in their marriage she had tried hard to get to know Padraic as he truly was beneath the facade of sophistication and brilliance. Her every attempt had been adroitly blocked, until she had finally given up, thinking that perhaps there really wasn't anything more. But always she had known better.

"Tell me," she said softly.

He took a deep breath and let it out slowly. "You know I grew up in Dublin and came to this country when I was eighteen. What I never told you was how damn poor my family was. Tinkers, we were called, and I suppose Tinkers we were, since we were always moving from one place to another trying to stay ahead of the rent collector. Dad worked when he happened to be in the mood; more often than not he preferred spending his time at the bottom of a bottle. Ma did the best she could, but it was too much for her. She walked out when I was ten, and that's the last any of us saw of her."

"Oh, Padraic... I'm so sorry...."

His face hardened for an instant, then relented. She could almost see him fighting against the instinct to close her out. For the first time she glimpsed where that came from.

"I got over being sorry about it a long time ago," he said. "Around the time I began to realize that this gift I have... or curse, whichever seems more apt at the moment...wouldn't be the same if I'd grown up in a nice genteel family. Self-pity isn't my problem, thank God, but I do seem to have a problem with looking on the brighter side of life and really believing it exists."

"I can see why now." Hesitant about probing too far, but anxious to know more, she asked, "Why did you decide to come to the States?"

He smiled wryly. "Mainly because that's where the ship I was on happened to dock. I signed up on a freighter when I was fifteen. They weren't too particular about papers, and I was big for my age. In the next three years I saw most of the world. By the time we hit New Orleans with a load of pipe fittings, I was ready to move on."

"You never mentioned any of that, either."

"I was ashamed of it," he said bluntly. At her incredulous look he went on. "Try to see it from my point of view. There you were, the sheltered granddaughter of two fine, loving people, and there I was, ex-tinker's brat, ex-stevedore, ex-jack-of-all-trades turned playwright. I was eight years older than you, but there seemed to be at least a couple of centuries between us in experience. I was terrified of hurting or disillusioning you, and in the end I managed to do both."

"Knowing the truth about you wouldn't have caused either," she murmured. "It was being kept in the dark that led to problems."

"I'm sorry, Mollie."

"Don't be," she said. "If there's anything I've learned over the last few years its that regrets are always futile." Her eyes met his across the table. "I think you know that, too."

"I do," he agreed, "but there are still times when I wish things had been different between us."

So did she, but she had meant what she said about not looking back. How much better it was to concentrate on the present. With a smile she picked up her spoon and began to eat the bouillabaisse, pausing only to compliment him on it. After a moment Padraic followed suit.

The fire sent a warm glow through the room. O'Casey lay at their feet, his long snout resting on his paws. Tiny lights on the Christmas tree twinkled brightly. Outside the snow continued to fall, heavier than before, but inside there was peace and comfort.

After dinner Padraic and Mollie cleared up, then settled in front of the fire with their glasses and the remains of the wine. Mollie had kicked off her shoes and curled her long legs under her. She was feeling pleasantly drowsy, but not yet ready for sleep.

"This is very nice," she murmured, almost to herself.

Seated beside her, close though not touching, Padraic smiled. "It is that. I can't remember the last time I felt so relaxed."

"Me either." The world she had left only a few hours before—of crowded city streets, the constant demands of her business, her own persona as a self-made professional—all seemed very far away. She viewed it with some befuddlement, as though unsure whether it was real or a briefly imagined dream.

That was nonsense, of course. Undoubtedly the product of her fatigue, the wine, the shock of being with Padraic. If anything, this was the dream. She would be only half surprised to wake up in her apartment and discover that she had never left New York.

"What are you thinking about?" Padraic asked.

"Dreams. How lovely they are ... exciting, but safe."

"Is this a dream?"

Mollie frowned slightly. "Don't you know?"

"Logically it's real. But what has logic to do with anything?"

She looked into the fire, than back to him. "Too complicated. Either it is a dream or it isn't."

"And if it is?" He had moved closer. She could feel the warmth of his big, hard body reaching out to her, supplanting the warmth of the fire, which seemed somehow to be growing hazy and far away.

The couch they sat on was wrapped in shadows, giving it an insubstantial form well suited to dreams.

If it was...? How would she feel then? To throw off the shackles of reality was an enticement she could scarcely resist. After so many years of having to be relentlessly pragmatic, the chance to indulge long-suppressed needs beckoned seductively.

Her lips parted soundlessly and, without knowing, she moistened them with the tip of her tongue.

Padraic's mouth tightened. He reached out and took her glass from her unresisting hand, setting it on the table beside his own. "Mollie, do you have an idea what it's doing to me to be so close to you and not know if I should...?"

"Should what?" Was that her voice, so soft and caressing? She put a hand to the back of her neck and absently lifted the thick weight of her hair. How green Padraic's eyes were. She could fall into them forever and never land. Like Alice through the looking glass, into another time and place. A dream.

A low groan broke from him. He bent his head, and his mouth touched hers, hot and yearning, savoring the softness of her lips. Unthinkingly she responded. Her hair drifted again over her shoulders as she reached out to him, cupping the back of his head, fingers tangling in rough ebony silk, drawing him closer.

Well-remembered and long-missed pleasure rippled through her. She knew what was happening was crazy; she should call a halt immediately. But somehow she couldn't bring herself to do it.

What was the harm, really? She wasn't involved with anyone else, hadn't been since her divorce, despite sporadic attempts to feel something for another man. And there was no evidence of another woman in Padraic's life; if there was one, at least she wasn't living with him.

Who would be hurt if they made love, just this once? His mouth had drifted down to her long, slender throat, and against his lips he felt the ripple of her laughter. His head jerked up. "You find this funny?"

"No, not exactly. I was only thinking that we should wait for New Years. You know, for auld lang syne."

"I don't want to wait," he said. "And I don't think you do, either." As though to prove his point his big hands cupped her breasts, feeling through the soft wool of her dress and the lace of her bra the hardened proof of her arousal.

"Did you know," he went on silkily, "that I was always fascinated by your nipples? They're such a delicate shade of pink and so incredibly responsive."

Mollie could feel herself blushing all the way down to the part of her in question. In an effort to right the balance she ran her hands over his chest and nipped lightly at his chin. "I could go on about how fascinated I was by your body, but I wouldn't want to embarrass you."

"That's all right," he assured her hastily. "I can stand it."

"Well then . . ." The words she murmured in his ear, contrary to his assurances, made him flush darkly. Before she had said all that was on her mind he grasped her waist and lowered her onto the couch.

Giddy with hunger and the intoxicating sense of her own power, Mollie smiled up at him. "I'll have you know we're in the process of crushing a very expensive dress."

"Can't have that," Padraic said, his voice low and raw with need. Before she could take another breath he had adeptly unzipped the dress and lowered it from her shoulders. "Sit up a little."

Mutely she obeyed, and the garment was stripped from her and tossed over the back of a chair. When she had dressed that morning it was with no expectation that anyone would see her half-naked. The bra and panties she had chosen were delicately feminine, as always. But she was also wearing panty hose, which she knew Padraic hated.

"I haven't changed my mind about these things," he said as he took hold of the waistband and pulled them down over her hips and thighs. He stopped for an instant, giving her a chance to object to his handling of her. When she did not, he finished removing the panty hose and tossed them on the floor.

Looming over her, he began to unbutton his shirt. She lay against the cushions and watched him, aware that her breath was coming fast and hard, causing her breasts to rise above the narrow cups of her bra and threaten to spill over.

Padraic was equally aware of the danger, and the temptation. He managed to withstand it long enough to get his shirt off and undo his belt, but then he had to pause and give his driving need release.

"This thing isn't locked, is it?" he demanded as he reached behind her to fumble with the catch of her bra.

"I don't think so," she assured him breathlessly. When it still wouldn't give after a moment she raised herself slightly and, replacing his hands with hers, undid the clasp. The lacy fabric fell away from her, revealing her breasts to his hungry eyes.

"Lord," he whispered, "you're every bit as beautiful as I remember."

"You aren't bad yourself," she managed huskily. Hardly aware of what she was doing, she rubbed against him, feeling the rough texture of his chest hair on her swollen nipples.

"I can't stand much more of this," he murmured.

"Then don't."

Their eyes met, his questioningly, hers still with a hint of uncertainty, but also with conviction. Whatever happened afterward, whatever the regrets or consequences, she could not leave him now any more than he could leave her.

Standing up swiftly, he removed the rest of his clothes and stood before her proudly naked. The sheer strength of him gave her a moment's pause, but that faded instantly and she reached out to him.

With a groan he came to her, his head burrowing into the warmth between her breasts even as his hands removed her last garment. When the final barrier was gone they moved together artlessly.

Their joining was swift; neither could bear to wait a heartbeat longer. But for Mollie it was also slightly painful. Padraic felt her flinch and stopped, lifting himself above her. His eyes were dark, clouded with mingled desire and concern, as he stared into hers.

"Mollie . . . are you all right?"

"Yes," she assured him quickly. "It's just that I haven't . . . that is, it's been a long time for me."

"How long?" The words were out before he could stop them. Even as he cursed himself inwardly, knowing that he had no right to ask, he couldn't help being filled by a burgeoning sense of elation.

"Since you," she said, and gasped when he reflexively moved within her. "I tried, God knows, but I couldn't."

"I'm glad," he said fiercely. "Forgive me, but I am." Then he moved again, and she forgot everything except the overwhelming pleasure he was bringing her and, at its end the blinding joy of absolute release.

Chapter Four

The first thing Mollie saw when she opened her eyes the next morning was the poinsettia on the dresser. She stared at it blankly for several moments until the implications of where she was sank in. Then she sat up abruptly.

The covers fell away to reveal that she was naked. She grabbed for them hastily, even though she was alone and likely to remain so. Padraic had seemed to understand the night before that she needed time by herself to come to terms with what had happened. He had acquiesced to her sleeping in the guest room, though she knew he would have preferred her to share his.

Had she done so they would undoubtedly have made love again, which would only have left her with more problems to sort out.

She had more than enough as it was. Wrapped in her robe, she slipped out the door, listened for a moment, then hurried into the bathroom. A hot shower helped to restore her equilibrium a little, but nothing could banish the sense of unreality that pursued her from the night before.

When she returned to her room and dressed in a pair of warm wool slacks and a bulky sweater, she knew that she was choosing the clothes as much for their lack of allure as their practicality. That done, she began to brush her hair, only to break off when her glance fell on what lay beyond her windows.

Snow. A great deal of it. Stretching as far as the eye could see, weighing down the trees, gathering in immense drifts, blowing on the brisk wind, and still falling. A blizzard's worth, firmly ending any tentative idea she might have had about staging a quick exit.

With a harried grimace she went downstairs. The sounds she'd heard earlier had stopped, and now there was only silence in the house. Puzzled, she poked her head into the kitchen and found it empty. A coffeepot sat on a low flame on the stove; otherwise there was no sign of Padraic.

O'Casey's ecstatic woof drew her to the back door. She opened it and peered out. A path had been shoveled from the kitchen to the woodshed a short distance away. As she watched Padraic appeared from around the other side, wheeling a cartload of logs. When he saw her, he stopped and frowned.

"You shouldn't be standing in the door like that. It's too cold. Go back inside."

Mollie bristled at his authoritarian tone. It grated on her independent nature, not to mention provid-

ing a severe letdown from his loving behavior of the
night before. "I'm fine," she informed him tartly.
"I see it snowed."

"Very good," he drawled. "Ever think of becoming a meteorologist?"

She flushed and whirled around, storming back
inside and slamming the door behind her. Where
did he get off being so sarcastic with her? Furi-
ously she blinked back tears, telling herself that she
was a fool to care what he thought. But after what
they had shared his derision was even harder to take
than she could have imagined.

She was still trembling when the door opened
behind her, and a moment later she felt a warm,
firm hand on her arm. "I'm sorry, Mollie. I don't
know what got into me."

Refusing to look at him, she shrugged. "It
doesn't matter."

"Of course it does." Insistently, despite her half
hearted resistance, he turned her around and gently lifted her chin so that she had no choice but to
meet his eyes. "What happened last night was so
beautiful that it threw me. I woke up this morning
not sure of anything except that I wished we could
have gone on as we were forever. That scared the
hell out of me, and I took it out on you the first
chance I got."

His honesty soothed her, enough so that she was
driven to match it. "I was scared, too."

He laughed softly. "We're a pair."

An odd choice of words, she thought, but undeniably apt. Or at least it had been during the five years of their marriage, and again last night. But that was all, she reminded herself. What had passed between them in the hours of darkness had been a dream, nothing more. To forget that would be to open the way for pain greater than any she had yet experienced.

"Are we snowed in?" she managed to ask.

He nodded. "The electricity and phone are out. We can figure it will be at least a couple of days before the roads are cleared." At her quick look of concern he added, "There's nothing to worry about. We've got plenty of food, and there's an auxiliary generator to run the water pump. As far as keeping warm goes," he said smiling, "we'll have to use our ingenuity."

"Let's use that wood you brought in instead," she suggested with some asperity.

He chuckled, but didn't press the matter, and a few minutes later she saw him feeding bits of tinder into the cast iron stove that stood at the opposite end of the kitchen from the fireplace. "This will work better than an open fire," he explained, "though I'll start that, too."

Mollie nodded, but otherwise didn't respond. She was afraid that if she tried to speak her voice would give away the fact that she had been surreptitiously watching him while she prepared breakfast. The graceful movements of his large, muscular body had never failed to fascinate her. When he straightened up and brushed off his hands she hastily looked away.

"Breakfast is ready."

"Good," he said. "I'm starved."

So was she, though she told herself it was because of the cold. In fact she knew perfectly well that vigorous lovemaking had always increased her appetite. Padraic knew it, too; he grinned as she helped herself to a second slice of toast and liberally spread it with raspberry jam.

"Hungry?" he asked mildly as he held out the plate of crisp bacon.

"A little." To substantiate that claim she forced herself to take only one strip instead of the three or four she would have liked. Since she had cooked so much that left a considerable pile on the plate, but Padraic made short work of that, as he did of the toast and the fluffy scrambled eggs—to which she had added a hint of dill before realizing that she had done so because he liked them that way.

"You were always a great cook," he said as he sat back, replete at last.

"I managed. Are you sure you had enough?" She looked pointedly at the array of empty plates. He had a nerve being able to eat like that and not put any weight on.

"Worrying about your waistline?"

His uncanny ability to read her thoughts had always disconcerted her, but never more so than now. "No," she said as she stood up and began to clear the table.

Padraic rose and gestured her back into her chair. "I'll do it. Have another cup of coffee and relax."

She wanted to say that she couldn't possibly relax with him so near, but stopped herself in time and managed to feign interest in an old magazine while he tidied up the kitchen. When he had finished he returned to her, saw what she was doing and shook his head. "I had no idea you were interested in commodities futures."

"What?"

"The article you're reading. It's about commodities trading, specifically futures." Lights danced in his emerald eyes as he realized he had caught her out. "I tried to make sense of it myself a few weeks ago without much luck. Maybe you could explain it to me."

"I'm afraid not. Padraic..."

He pulled out his chair and sat down beside her. "Yes?"

"We can't go on like this, dancing around each other." She took a deep breath. "Perhaps what happened last night shouldn't have, but I can't bring myself to really regret it. If you do, I'm sorry."

"I don't."

He spoke so softly that it took her a moment to understand what she had heard. Her eyes flew to his face. "Really?"

Padraic nodded somberly. "I'm glad it happened. No woman has ever meant as much to me as you do, and now I'm sure none ever will."

"I don't understand." He had spoken as though he still cared for her, as though no one else had ever mattered. But she knew that couldn't possibly be true. "What about Jessica?"

He flinched, and for a moment she thought he didn't mean to answer, but at length he said, "Jessica was . . . a mistake."

Mollie choked back a humorless laugh. "I suppose that's as good a word as any."

"I mean it. I used her to hurt you, because I was angry that you didn't trust me. As soon as I'd done it, I knew it was wrong, but it was already too late."

"I don't want to talk about it anymore." The mere thought of Jessica Peters—the beautiful, sensuous actress who was the toast of both Broadway and Hollywood—made her stomach twist painfully.

"I think we'd better."

"No." She started to rise, thinking only of getting away.

His hand lashed out, closing over her wrist in a grip that would have hurt if it hadn't eased so quickly. "Please, Mollie, give me a chance."

More even than the words, the anguish in his voice reached her. He was a proud man who had never begged for anything, yet she sensed that he would do so now if that was what it would take to make her listen. Humbled by his willingness to make so great an effort, she relented.

"It wasn't what you thought," he said when she sat down again. "Jessica was never my mistress."

"Are you saying you never slept with her?" Mollie demanded incredulously.

"No, I'm not. I slept with her, all right. What I'm saying is that I never made love with her, or had sex, or got involved, or however else you want to put it."

Mollie didn't believe him. She simply couldn't, after so much pain and disappointment. Yet neither could she completely ignore the ring of truth in his words. Whatever else Padraic might have been, he had never been a liar. Truth shone from the man himself as it did from his prose. Could that have changed, or was there a chance she had misjudged him?

"Tell me," she said, knowing even as she spoke the words that they should have uttered years before. "The night you spent with her, what happened?"

"You remember we were rehearsing *Winners and Losers*?" When she nodded, he went on. "The run-through went very late. Afterward we all went out to dinner. You and I had fought that morning about the same problem that had been at the crux of all our arguments. You wanted your own career; I wanted you to devote yourself to me. It was damn selfish on my part, I admit that. But at the time I didn't see it, and I was in no mood to start up with you again. Anyway, after the others left I stayed on at the restaurant with Jessica. After a while she suggested we go to her apartment."

Good old Jessica, Mollie thought glumly. She could picture the other woman seeing her opportunity and not hesitating to grab it.

"Neither one of us was feeling any pain when we got to her place," Padraic said. "We sat on the couch, still talking. She was easy to be with, beautiful, intelligent—" he smiled slightly "—admiring of me and my work. She took me very seriously, did old Jessie."

"So you went to bed with her?"

"With the worst intentions. I fully planned to give her everything she wanted and them some. After all, it had been quite a while since you and I had made love, and I was more than ready."

"I see," Mollie said. "But then how can you claim that you didn't . . . ?"

"Because, sweet love, Mother Nature—no accident she's female—always has a few tricks up her sleeve where would-be wayward husbands are concerned. There I was, all primed for action, and suddenly, there I wasn't. If you get my meaning."

Mollie did, though it took a moment. She had always found Padraic to be an incredible lover, strong, tender, giving, and unfailingly virile. Exactly as he had been the night before. To think that he hadn't been able to perform with a woman took some getting used to.

"Does this have anything to do with why you left New York?" she asked.

"Did I flee in horror of my lost manhood?"

She flushed, but nodded.

"No, it wasn't that at all. I left when I realized you were convinced I'd been unfaithful to you."

Her eyes closed briefly, reflecting hurtful memories. "Davey Benson called me that morning, after you'd been out all night. Remember him?"

"Vividly. Last I heard he was doing toilet cleaner commercials."

Mollie giggled. "That's about what he deserves. He loved every minute of telling me that you were with Jessica. He even gave me her address and said if I didn't believe him, I should go see for myself."

"So you did."

She nodded grimly. All too well she remembered the moment when Jessica had answered the door

clad only in a sheer nightie and languidly beckoned her inside, just as Padraic walked out of the
bedroom.

They had stared at each other for a long, agoniz-
ing moment before Mollie had turned and run for
her very life.

"I should have waited," she murmured, "to hear
what you had to say."

"I thought so, too, at the time, but since then
I've come to see it in a different perspective. The
fact that I hadn't actually made love to Jessica
didn't mean that I hadn't failed you. I had, and in
the process I'd failed myself." He laughed harshly.
"With hindsight I even know why it all happened."

"Why?" Mollie said softly.

"For months I'd felt my life slipping away from
me. I was being seduced by my own success and
didn't realize it. What had once sustained me, the
straightforward compulsion to tell a tale, was no
longer enough. I wanted money, fame, adulation,
and believed them all to be my right. Against all this
stood you, with your own problems about my success, yet also a continual reminder that there was a
great deal more to life."

"I didn't mean to hold you back in any way."

"You didn't. On the contrary, without you I
would never have gone as far as I did. I found that
out after we separated, when nothing seemed

worthwhile. So I came here, first to lick my wounds, then to rediscover myself. I bought the farmhouse because I told myself it happened to be convenient. But in fact I missed you terribly and felt closer to you here."

Mollie closed her eyes against the tears that were threatening to fall. A piercing sense of sadness filled her. If only she and Padraic had been so honest with each other in the past, they would never have come to such a point. All the pain and regret of the last few years could have been avoided.

"Don't," Padraic said. He touched her cheek gently with the back of his hand in a gesture she remembered all too well. "There's no point in thinking about what might have been. The past is the only thing we can't change."

"It's just that..." She broke off and took a deep breath, fighting for control. What she had to say was hard enough without breaking down in the middle. "I was in love with you. Really in love. I thought we would be together for the rest of our lives, and when I realized that wasn't going to happen it was almost more than I could bear."

"You came out of it all right, though. The success you've had since shows that."

"Don't be fooled," she said. "I'm proud of what I've accomplished, but I know a lot of it happened because I felt driven to fill the enormous hole in my life after you were gone."

He shook his head in bewilderment. "I thought you'd always wanted your own business."

"So I did, but not quite to the extent I've achieved." She made a sound halfway between a laugh and a sob. "A claim could be made that I've overdone it."

"Is that how you feel?"

"I don't know," she admitted. "There are days when everything goes great and I'm on top of the world. Then there are times when there are loads of problems, but I feel a great deal of satisfaction in dealing with them. But once in a while—" she smiled wanly "—I wake up in the middle of the night wondering why on earth I'm bothering. What's the point?"

He nodded slowly. "I know what you mean. It's happened to me, too."

"How could it have? Your writing is your life."

"Was," he corrected. "Not anymore."

A chill ran through her. If Padraic had lost his tremendous gift, something truly important had gone out of the world. "But you said you were still working."

"I am, and the irony of it is that the results are better than ever. The difference is that they don't satisfy me the way they once did."

"Do you know why that is?" If he had found the answer, perhaps he could share it with her.

"Yes, I know."

"Why?"

He looked at her for a long moment, then smiled gently. "Later, sweetheart. We'll talk about it later. In the meantime, let's go out and play."

Chapter Five

"In the snow?" Mollie asked.

"Of course. How could we pass it up?" He rose and held out a hand to her. "We'll make angels and build a snowman. And if that isn't serious enough for you, we can put out food for the animals. With this bad storm, they'll need it."

Within an hour Mollie was flushed and laughing. Snowflakes clung to her eyelashes and the wisps of hair escaping from beneath the knit hat Padraic had insisted she wear. He had even rummaged around and found her a pair of mittens that looked vaguely familiar to her.

"I left these here, too, didn't I?" she asked when they were catching their breath after hauling out and spreading several bales of hay, as well as what seemed like at least half a ton of nuts and seed.

He nodded, his eyes glowing from the exertion and something else she didn't quite want to recognize. "They were in a drawer."

"Why didn't you throw them out?"

"Never got around to it, I guess."

Mollie didn't believe him, but that was all right. The snow was beginning to taper off, and patches of blue sky showed through the clouds. It was very cold, and the air had a crystalline quality that made every sound reverberate in a high, sweet way.

With much laughing and teasing they built a snowman who turned out to be slightly lopsided but still perfectly respectable. They made angels in the snow. Padraic had a hard time getting back onto his feet without mussing them; Mollie had to show him how. When she held out her hand, he took it and tugged.

"Oooff."

"Sorry, sweetheart, I couldn't resist."

Lying on her back, she stared up at him. His skin was ruddy with the cold, and his eyes gleamed brightly. A pulse beat in his jaw, which she suspected had nothing to do with their exertions.

Memories of the previous night flitted through her mind. She parted her lips and sighed softly.

He held himself above her a moment longer, big and hard, yet not in the least threatening. Her last coherent thought before his mouth covered hers with fierce demand was that she was a match for him.

His tongue searched her moist warmth with devastating thoroughness. He filled her with the taste and scent of him, evoking all the while an even more intimate possession. Through the barriers of their heavy clothes she could feel his arousal. A low, yearning moan broke from her as her hands tangled in his thick hair, holding him even closer.

When he moved she did not know, but one instant she was lying beneath him, pressed into the snow, and the next their positions had been reversed. She rested on his broad chest, looking down at him bemusedly. He smiled so tenderly that for a moment her heart stopped. Without thinking she initiated a kiss that in its own way was as powerfully sensual as the one they had just shared.

When it was over they were both breathing hard. Mollie felt taken aback, even embarrassed. Now that she thought about it, she realized that she had never been the aggressor in their lovemaking. Perhaps because of the difference in their ages and experience, that role had always fallen to Padraic. By the time they might have changed, the habit was solidly set.

He saw the hesitation in her eyes and stood up, without any difficulty this time, drawing her with him. They gave a great deal of attention to brushing the snow off each other's backs, which effectively did away with any unease and led to a mad chase back to the house.

"Hot chocolate," he announced when they were back inside. "In front of the fire. I might even be able to find a few marshmallows to toast."

"Who could ask for anything more?"

They did an off-key rendition of the song of the same name, making up most of the words as they went along. O'Casey lay down on the floor and eyed them mournfully.

"Sorry, boy," Mollie said, petting him apologetically. "We'll cut it out."

"Remember when we used to sing in the shower?" Padraic asked as he took a saucepan from the cupboard and poured milk into it.

"Uh...I suppose." She was blushing, but hoped he would think it was from the cold.

"Suppose? Those are some of the fondest memories of my life."

Mollie broke down and grinned. "There were times when I thought I was doomed to pruneyness."

"You made a terrific-looking prune, honey. Believe me."

"Hmm, you weren't so bad yourself. Now do you mind if we change the subject?"

"Yes, but I can live with it. How about some music?"

Mollie agreed, and he stuck a tape in the stereo. Soft Christmas music filled the room.

"Do you mind?" he asked.

"No, I guess I'm in more of a holiday mood than I thought."

"Me too."

"It's nice, isn't it?" she said, looking at the tree, but seeing him.

"Yes, I can see now why people do this regularly." He sat down beside her and handed her a steaming cup of cocoa.

She took a sip and giggled. "I was just thinking how angry I was at Jerry when he messed up my reservation at the inn, and now I'm glad he did."

"Uh . . . sweetheart, there's something I have to tell you about that."

She cast him a long look through her lashes. "Oh, really?"

"Since I've been living here Jerry's gotten to be a good friend."

"How nice."

"He knew I missed you."

"Did he by any chance mention I was coming up?"

"I believe he did. Only in passing, mind you."

"Funny thing," Mollie said, "about those people who decided to stay on longer than they'd planned. You know, the ones Jerry couldn't bring himself to put out."

"There weren't any."

"What's that?"

"The people, they didn't exist. I asked Jerry to tell you there was no room."

Mollie sighed and licked a trace of cocoa from her upper lip. "Devious of you."

"I was desperate."

"Never, not you."

"Really, I was. The moment I heard you were coming back I knew I had to see you, and more than that, I wanted us to really have a chance to talk. It seemed like a godsend until I realized you'd be staying at the inn and there was no reason for us to even run into each other."

"I have to tell you the truth, Padraic. I'm enormously touched that you went to such lengths."

"Really?"

She nodded solemnly. "It's very flattering."

"Well, good. I was afraid you might be annoyed."

"Because you manipulated me?"

He groaned softly. "You are annoyed."

The smile she gave him, soft and lingering, assured him that she was anything but. "You've turned into a romantic."

"My deep, dark secret and you blurt it out."

"I'm sure O'Casey is shocked."

He got up, tossed another log on the fire and returned to her. Silence reigned, except for the crackle and hiss of the flames. At length, without looking at her, he said, "I want you back, Mollie. I want us to try again."

She had always imagined that if she ever heard those words she would be on top of the world. What divorced woman didn't occasionally fantasize about a repentant ex-husband longing for a reconciliation? But that was all it was, the stuff of dreams, with no connection to reality.

Softly, she said, "We've changed a great deal, Padraic."

"For the better."

"Maybe, but we've done it separately. You're not the man I married, and I'm certainly not the woman you chose as your wife."

"We're still the same people," he insisted. "We've simply learned a few things along the way."

"It's true the last few years have been very...educational. For one thing, I've learned that I need a great deal of independence. I've gotten used to making my own decisions and going my own way without having to consider anyone else. Not only that, but I've discovered that I like that kind of freedom."

"You were telling me that you wondered sometimes if it was all worthwhile."

"Everyone has dark moments of self-doubt. I'm no different in that respect. What I'm saying is that I could never go back to the way I used to be, subordinating my own needs to someone else's."

"Namely mine."

Sadly, she nodded. "It wasn't your fault. For a long time I blamed you, but now I know better. I was so young, and so uncertain, that it was easiest for me to try to live through you."

"Plenty of women do that with their husbands."

"And I doubt if one of them has ever been truly happy. No, it wasn't for me. Wasn't and isn't."

"There's no reason to think it would happen again," he said.

"But the potential is there, and it scares the daylights out of me."

He put down his cup and turned to her, taking her face between his big hands and looking directly into her eyes. "Ask yourself this, mavourneen," he said, his voice taking on a soft burr. "Are you really afraid of me, or of yourself?"

Through stiffened lips she murmured, "Is this a trick question?"

He laughed and dropped a soft kiss on her mouth. "No tricks, not now and not ever. But I meant what I said. I hurt you, so it's natural for you to be afraid, but you have far more control over this situation than you think."

"Last night," she reminded him, "I had no control at all."

He sat back and regarded her steadily. "Is that what troubles you?"

"It was exactly as it had always been, you leading and me following. Not," she added hastily, "that I minded. It was beautiful and . . . thrilling."

"Thank you," he said gravely. "However, it can't have been a complete success if it left you with such doubts."

"Was that the purpose, to erase all my doubts and make me agreeable to anything you wanted?"

"In part," he admitted disarmingly. "I'm a man, not a saint. I want you, and I'm not overly scrupulous about how I get you."

"Thanks for the warning."

"As though you needed it. You understand me better than you think."

"It's true that I understand enough to be afraid," she said.

"Because of last night?"

When she nodded, he sighed deeply. "I didn't mean that to happen. I'd told myself that I'd be the soul of patience. But once you were actually here, so close to me, I couldn't restrain myself."

"Don't sound so regretful. As I said, it was good."

"Not if you're frightened off."

The music stopped. In the sudden silence Mollie could hear her heart thudding ominously. She was coming face-to-face with truths she wasn't necessarily ready to confront. Truths about herself even more than about Padraic. Honesty forced her to admit that was the true source of her fear.

"My grandparents," she said suddenly, "were very good to me."

"So you've always said."

"It's a shame they died before you could meet them. They would both have liked you, and I think you would have felt the same way about them."

"I'm sure I would have, but..."

"But what's that got to do with anything?"

"Obviously something. Will you explain it to me?"

She was willing enough to try, which was more than she had ever done in the past. Slowly she said, "You know my parents were killed when I was eight?"

He nodded. "In a car accident. A terrible tragedy."

"Yes, it was, and not only because they were my parents. They were also very good people, and so much in love." She smiled wistfully. "That's what I remember most about them, the love that was always present, a steady, constant glowing like a warm fire through all the days and nights."

"They were very fortunate, though I'm sure they worked at it."

"Yes," she said. "Looking back, I can see that they did. In a way I suppose their dying together was merciful, since they would have been utterly devastated apart. As Grania and Da were."

"They died shortly before we met?"

"That's right, within a few months of each other. And again I told myself it was for the best, because they also shared a great love. It was different in some ways from what I saw with my parents, probably since it'd had so many more years in which to ripen. But at bottom the effect was the same.''

''Did you feel shut out by the love they shared?'' he asked gently.

She shook her head, not offended by the question, because she had accepted that he was genuinely trying to understand. ''There was never anything like that, either with my parents or with Grania and Da. I really believe that the more you love, the greater your capacity to do so. They lived at the center of a magic circle, and they didn't hesitate to let me in.''

The beginnings of comprehension shone in Padraic's emerald eyes. ''At least not until they died and the love went away.''

Why was she surprised that he had gotten the point so quickly? At the heart of his great talent lay an ability to uncover the most private and even painful sources of human motivation, to strip the soul bare and shine the light of reason on it. Once that had seemed so callous to her that she had instinctively shied away from ever being the object of his penetrating interest, but now she saw it in different terms, realizing that his understanding was not a threat but a gift.

''It took me years to see the problem,'' she said, ''and even then I refused to deal with it. I did love you, even though that filled me with fear, but when you seemed to withdraw from me, I accepted it without a fight because that was what I'd been expecting to happen all along."

"And I was too obtuse to realize it," he said in self-disgust.

"It wasn't your fault," she insisted, reaching out to him. "Perhaps if we'd been genuinely open with each other during our marriage I might have expected you to understand. But I'd done everything possible to keep you from really seeing inside me."

"And I'd done the same."

They exchanged a slow, sad smile. "As you said," she murmured, "we're a pair."

"None of which means things wouldn't be different if we tried again."

"I don't know, Padraic. After all this time, all that water under the bridge... Not to belabor the point, but we aren't the same people."

"Isn't that to our advantage?"

She didn't know. There was no easy answer to what he was asking. Knowing the source of her fears didn't mean that she had done away with them. She still remembered all too clearly how desperately hurt she had been, and she had a natural disinclination to risk such pain again. Especially with a man as overwhelming as Padraic.

"I have a friend," she said softly. "Her name's

Joanna; she's a former model turned actress. Anyway, she has a theory that career women can't have successful relationships with men who are either their own age or older. She believes the conflicts are simply too profound and that it's smarter to get a younger man, one who's grown up with the idea of the liberated woman and has far fewer problems dealing with it."

"Does she practice what she preaches?" Padraic asked, the merest suggestion of a growl in his voice.

"She has, several times, but lately..."

"Yes..." He was smiling as though he already knew what she was going to say.

"She met someone older whom she really likes, too much, in fact, at least to hear her tell it. He's forty, a banker, very strong-willed, and no matter how hard she tries, she can't seem to tear herself away from him."

"Because he's a man," Padraic said succinctly, "not a pet. If you want fuzzy warm affection, get a dog. No offense, O'Casey. For anything more substantial you have to take some risks."

"I know all about risks." She couldn't help it, she was getting angry. He seemed intent on challenging her. "But there are good risks and bad, as with everything else in life. Only a fool ignores past experiences instead of learning from them."

He ran a hand through his hair, already unruly from the wind outside. She stifled an impulse to smooth the stray strands and kept her attention on the fire instead.

"Which leaves us where?" he said.

"I don't know." She wished to God that she did.

Padraic stood up and walked over to the windows. The light was beginning to fade, along with his hopes. "It's stopped snowing."

Her hand on his arm startled him; he hadn't heard her come to his side. "I'm sorry," she said softly. "I'd like nothing better to be able to tell you that all this has worked and I want us to start over again. But if I said that, I'd be pretending to be a lot more certain than I really am, which I don't think you would really want."

"No," he agreed, "I wouldn't, but don't imagine for a moment that I'm giving up."

"Never," she assured him. "I know how tenacious you can be."

"Especially when something very important to me is at stake."

Thrilled though she was by the suggestion that he wanted her so much, Mollie managed to smile lightly. But the smile faded and was replaced by an expression of puzzlement as she said, "Listen. Do you hear that?"

For a moment he didn't; then his face, too, was wreathed in amazement. "Is that what I think it is?"

"Sleigh bells."

"It isn't even dark yet. What's Santa doing out this early?"

"Unless I miss my guess...." She opened the window and peered out, heedless of the brisk wind that was blowing the snow into fanciful swirls of glittering white. "Look," she said, pointing. "It's the old sleigh from the Rooster Inn. Jerry's father used to get it out every Christmas, but it's been in mothballs for years."

"Not anymore, apparently."

They both hurried to the door in time to see the large, horse-drawn sleigh pull up in front. A red-faced, slightly abashed-looking Jeremiah Withers waved a hand in greeting. "Hope I'm not interrupting anything."

"Not at all," Padraic assured him, staring in amazement at the prancing horses and the shiny sleigh. "That looks like fun."

"It is. Hop in."

"Us? But...?"

"No buts," Jerry said firmly. "I've been rounding up everyone for hours. You're the last. We're all getting together at the inn for caroling before church. It won't be the same without you."

Padraic and Mollie exchanged a startled look. "That's for sure," she said. "Obviously you've never heard us sing."

Jerry grinned broadly. "Doesn't matter. It's the thought that counts."

The horses shied, eager to be on their way. "Coming?" Jerry asked.

"Who could pass it up?" Mollie said with a laugh. Padraic hurried inside to get their coats, then helped her into the sleigh. They snuggled together under a blanket.

The last of the storm clouds had fled, and in the crystal-clear sky they could see the first few stars announcing the arrival of Christmas Eve.

Chapter Six

By the time they reached the inn it was fully dark. The sky had turned into black velvet across which a giant hand had tossed an infinity of glittering diamonds. Snow crunched under their feet as they walked up the path. Inside, a roaring fire cast warmth over the crowd of people gathered around the piano. Mollie spotted several familiar faces. She waved in response to their greetings and joined Padraic at the punch bowl.

"I'd forgotten how much fun this is," she said. "It's wonderful."

He smiled down at her, the look in his eyes so warm and tender that she flushed. "You're as happy as a child, aren't you? Full of all the magic of the moment."

She nodded slowly. "I suppose I am. Does it seem foolish to you?"

"Not at all. In fact," he said as he glanced up at the ceiling, "I'm all for the holiday spirit."

Mollie followed the direction of his gaze and laughed. "Mistletoe. I might have known."

"You wouldn't want to fool with tradition, would you?"

She fluttered her eyelashes innocently. "Who, me? Wouldn't dream of it."

But the teasing faded when he touched her lips with his, first gently, then with increasing demand until the sights and sound of the party faded away and there were only the two of them, afloat in a world of pure sensation.

They stood inches apart, not touching at any point except with their lips, but in the space between them a powerful current flowed. Mollie had a distant image of electrified air, glowing with a force she could not define but felt she knew intimately.

When they at last broke apart, reluctantly, the strange sense of ethereal contact went on, even after they were both swept into the crowd of people around the piano, who kindly did not joke about their preoccupation with one another.

Years had passed since Mollie had last sung carols, and she suspected Padraic had never done so. But there was tolerance for rusty voices, and batches of sheet music for faulty memories.

They sang all the old favorites, from the jovial "God Rest Ye Merry, Gentlemen" to the tender "Silent Night." In between the singing they drank punch and eggnog, nibbled on Christmas cookies and fruitcake, and talked.

Mollie caught up on news from old friends. She chatted with Mabel Porter, who ran a local gift shop when she wasn't painting, and with Carly Phillips, whom she had gone to school with and who had since become a vet. Norris Daniels was there, another schoolmate, who had followed his father into the family law firm. There were others, too, easily a dozen in all that she knew but hadn't seen in several years.

To her surprise they were all well acquainted with Padraic and accepted him as one of their own. He fitted in easily with the happy crowd, in some ways more easily than she did after having been away so long.

Shortly before midnight they all piled into the assortment of sleighs and sleds waiting outside the inn and made the short trek to the church. It was a small, white clapboard building, set in a copse of old oak trees, with a graceful bell tower and pretty stained glass windows. Built in the early eighteenth century, it had changed little over the years.

To Mollie the church had always possessed a special quality of peace and reassurance that she had never found anyplace else. As she stood within the carved wooden doors, looking down the long aisle toward the altar, she realized that had not changed. Even the small children, entering in their parents' arms or with their hands securely tucked in larger ones, were awed and subdued by the atmosphere. The golden light reflecting off mellowed oak and muted glass seemed to say that here all earthly cares were put aside and a higher purpose ruled.

Instinctively Mollie took Padraic's arm as they walked down the aisle. He put his hand over hers, and they exchanged a smile.

The minister was a young man with unabashed enthusiasm for his calling who was clearly deeply moved by the significance of this particular night. He eloquently shared that with his congregation as he spoke in simple but evocative terms of the meaning of the child born into the world so long ago and so far away.

Mollie had never thought of herself as an especially religious person. She had fallen out of the habit of attending church regularly, and had frankly felt no lack in her life as a result. Over the years she had come to take her faith so much for granted that she rarely gave it any thought.

Padraic was the same. There had been a time in his life when cynicism and general weariness with the world made him skeptical about all religion. He had turned away from it without a qualm, and for quite some time had congratulated himself on not needing what he had tended to regard as a crutch.

With the passing of the years and the painful acquiring of wisdom his views had changed. He now had a sense of something larger than himself that breached the barriers of human frailty and solitude, and imbued him with a strength that he was honest enough to admit he would not have had on his own.

When the notes of the last "Amen" faded away Mollie and Padraic remained where they were for a long moment. They did not look at each other, nor did they speak but between them there flowed a current of understanding that was startling in both its clarity and familiarity. Though neither had experienced it before, both recognized it as another and deeper ramification of the passion they had shared. It was a spiritual celebration of what they had known physically, and made clear to them for the first time the full rightness of the expression "making love."

But powerful and moving as it was, it did not completely banish all doubts. At least, not for Mollie. No sooner did she leave the cloistered atmosphere of the church than a deadening sense of fear and confusion settled over her.

"Padraic," she said softly as the others were making their plans to return to various homes for present opening and partying, "Let's go back to the house."

She didn't need to say anything more. Like her, he needed the solitude in which they could gather their contrary thoughts and hopefully come to some resolution.

O'Casey greeted them ecstatically the instant they set foot in the door. He seemed to sense that something momentous was in the air. Only with difficulty did they get him calmed down enough to let them catch their breath.

Padraic struck a match to the fire he had laid earlier and poured them each a generous measure of brandy. Mollie had sat down on the couch. He started to take a place beside her, then changed his mind and settled in a nearby chair, facing her.

At her quizzical look he shrugged. "I'm trying hard not to pressure you, but if I get within touching distance I won't be responsible for my good intentions."

Mollie's mood had lifted somewhat since they returned to the house. She managed a gentle smile. "That's very flattering."

"It's also quite serious. I've already told you that I want you back and that I'm not overly scrupulous about how I go about achieving that."

The note of self-disgust in his voice surprised and distressed her. "You didn't use to be so critical of yourself," she said. "I seem to remember that you were always quite ruthless but never thought twice about it."

"I've changed."

"Yes, I know."

"You believe me now?"

"I think I did from the beginning," she said.

"Then why...?"

"Am I still so uncertain?"

When he nodded, she sighed deeply. The words to explain herself did not come easily. At length she said, "You seem so happy here."

She was a little envious of that, even as she understood how hard won his contentment must have been. That he believed he would be happier still if she stayed with him, she did not doubt. But even without her, he had done quite well.

Could she say the same for herself?

Yes, Mollie decided after a moment, she could. And that was important, because her success without him lay at the heart of her difficulty in contemplating a reconciliation.

"Padraic...I have a good life in New York."

"I hadn't presumed otherwise."

"What I mean is, it's very satisfying in many ways. My work, for instance, is very important to me, but it also takes a great deal of time and effort."

"As does anything worthwhile," he said. "Besides, it's what you always wanted to do."

She remembered that he had somehow known that before she did herself, but it had not meant that he could truly accept it. "I can't give up any of that."

He leaned forward, elbows resting on his knees, his hands clasped together. "Of course not. Surely you don't think I'd expect you to?"

"I don't know what you'd expect. When we were married everything revolved around your work. I didn't blame you for that," she went on hastily, "or at least, if I did, I got over it. Your work is important, but so is mine."

"You don't hear me arguing, do you?"

It couldn't be that easy. Could it? "Just like that, you accept my career, all the demands of my business and my independence? You won't have any trouble with any of that?"

"Of course I will," he said. "From time to time. But the point is that I approve of what you're doing. To be blunt about it, I'm damn relieved that you're making your own life instead of trying to live in the reflection of mine."

Before she could comment he added, "And while we're on the subject of work, I ought to tell you that what I'm doing these days is no piece of cake and there may be times when you resent it."

"Just what are you doing?" she asked carefully. In the past he had never wanted to talk about his work until it was completed. While it was in process the mere attempt to uncover any information had been met with stony silence. That, too, had apparently changed.

"A novel," he said, and at her startled look, he laughed. "Remember when I used to make fun of novelists?"

"I seem to recall your saying something about them being self-indulgent because they wrote without the discipline of either actors or audience."

"I meant it, too," he said ruefully. "Which I suppose means it's only just that I should now be joining them."

"How's it coming along?"

"Better than I have any right to expect, considering my prejudices. But there's lots of hard work ahead, which is fine. Mind you, I'm not saying that I'm through writing for the stage. Someday I might go back to it. But in the meantime I have more than enough to keep me occupied."

She could well believe that. As comfortable as she was with the idea of sitting down and designing an entire new fashion line, that was how far she was from understanding how a play or a novel could be written. "You must need a great deal of peace and quiet."

"I can see where that train of thought is leading," he said lightly, "so let me head it off quickly. A writer makes his own concentration; surroundings can't create it for him. Sure I can write here, but I can also write in an apartment in New York, or anywhere else I choose to."

"How about on a roller coaster?" she asked deadpan. "Could you write there?"

"Well, now, I suppose my penmanship might leave something to be desired. Would you mind telling me how you came up with that one?"

"Because that's what my life often seems to be these days, and if we got back together you'd be caught right smack in the middle of it."

Ever a man to appreciate an inventive turn of mind, Padraic laughed. "It won't work, Mollie. If I have to take a roller coaster I will, but I'd be more interested in seeing if I couldn't help you get off it now and again."

"I've tried," she said, "and it doesn't seem to work out too well." The corners of her mouth lifted sardonically. "After all, this trip was supposed to be a rest cure."

"The best laid plans..."

"Yours seem to have worked out fine." She couldn't help but sound a little bitter. He had manipulated her very neatly.

He raised an eyebrow. "Have they?"

"I'm here, aren't I?"

"For the short term, which is not what I want."

"What's that line in *Winners and Losers*? 'Don't speak to me of tomorrow; the moment is all.'"

He flushed slightly. "A bit pretentious, don't you think?"

"No, I didn't mean it like that. The feeling that nothing is real except the present is perfectly understandable. Most of us have trouble either remembering the past or envisioning the future."

"But not us?"

She shook her head rather sadly. "Remembering the past as clearly as I do makes me afraid of any future we might try to have together."

His eyes narrowed, hiding the emerald glints. "You never impressed me as a woman who could be moved by fear."

"Touché."

"Have you become that?"

"No," she said, "of course not. But I have learned caution. I ask what you want, and you say 'you.' One word, not even two syllables. It's a bit scant for trying to plan a life."

He nodded slowly. "A valid criticism. The Bard may have thought all the world was a stage and we but players on it, but sometimes a good third act curtain line isn't enough."

She was silent, waiting for him to go on. He did so slowly and carefully. "I suppose what I really want—or more correctly, what I'm hoping for—is that we will find some way to combine our lives. They never really were, you know, not even when we were married. We existed in separate spheres that, if they touched at all, only did so around the outer edges."

The image was so apt that Mollie found herself nodding vigorously even as she changed it slightly. "Not spheres, though. Bubbles, that finally burst."

He grinned admiringly. "Ah, Mollie mine, which one of us is the storyteller, I'm wondering? You've got a fine eye for imagery."

"I should hope so, considering that's what I deal in. At any rate, I agree with you; we never did put our lives together. Do you really believe we could do so now?"

Padraic nodded firmly. "I've told you that I can work as well in New York as here. In fact, if you wanted to, we could keep this place for occasional weekends."

"Oh, no," Mollie said. "I wouldn't want that. The fact is, I've been trying to spend less time on managing my business and more on what I enjoy most, namely the designing itself. Little by little I'm finding people to work for me whom I can really trust, and I'm learning to delegate authority."

His smile deepened with an eagerness that made her heart turn over. "Then there's no problem," he said.

"Wait." He had started to rise. In another moment he would be touching her, and she would be lost. "It's not that simple to me. This has all happened so fast. You've had months, maybe even longer, to grow accustomed to the idea of our getting back together. But it's completely new to me, and I need to think about it." Softly she added, "Alone."

He started to say something, then thought better of it. "All right."

Mollie walked a little distance away from the house. She was warmly bundled up against the cold, but suspected that she wouldn't have been aware of it anyway. Not when her mind was filled with such turbulent thoughts and her heart with such tumultuous emotions.

She stood at a crossroads in her life; the decision she made would shape not only her own future but Padraic's as well. The fact that she understood the source of her doubts and fears did not make them easy to dismiss. She had been hurt badly, and she had a natural reluctance to make herself vulnerable to such pain ever again.

Yet how could she live with herself if she turned her back on even the chance of love?

The night wind blew a swirl of snow from a nearby tree. She watched the flakes dance in intricate patterns of remarkable beauty that vanished in an instant. The elusive sense of sadness that had come over her after the service was returning. It was the melancholy of darkness and solitude, added to the weight of her own confusion.

She turned and looked back at the house. The curtains in the kitchen window were open. Through them she could see the Christmas tree, with its ornaments and twinkling lights. O'Casey was stretched out nearby, fast asleep in front of the fire. As she watched, Padraic rose from his chair and came to stand by the window, looking out.

She knew that he couldn't see her; the shadows of the trees near where she stood hid her from view. Yet she could almost feel his eyes touching her, filled with a yearning she could not ignore, if only because it was matched by her own.

Off in the distance the clear, high note of a church bell tolled the hour. It was Christmas morning. The single day of the year that had always meant more to her than any other had come again, as it had for almost two millenia as it would for countless time to come.

As a child she had delighted in the specialness of Christmas, all the beautiful objects and traditions kept apart from the rest of life and held intact for the celebration of that one day. Later she had come to see it in less material terms, deeply appreciating the sense of love that flowered in the cold of winter. Even if it was an idealized hope of what might be, it still spoke to the deepest human need for faith and caring.

She walked a short way into the woods and paused, looking up at the starlit sky. The greatest gift she had received from Christmas was that sense of love, which had sustained her even when she felt her own love for Padraic turning to ashes and blowing away on a bitter wind. But now she began to wonder if that was indeed what had happened.

The snowflakes she had watched dancing on the wind had seemed without substance, yet the essence of them had not vanished. It still existed in the piles of snow into which they had fallen. When they evaporated or melted it would still be present in the very fabric of the world, where nothing was ever destroyed.

Was love itself so ephemeral? She could not bring herself to believe that. Deep down inside was the knowledge that it, more than anything else, existed forever.

The child who had come into the world so long ago had carried that message. And, in the final moments of that earthly life, the message had been crystallized into a plea that weak and errant humanity be forgiven.

Forgiveness and love. They were intimately tied together; one could not exist without the other.

Mollie had known, and then rejected, her own capacity for love. Yet it remained strong within her. Forgiveness, however, was another matter. She had truly never thought much about it.

Now she did. The need was there, glowing within her with the white-hot intensity of truth. She had to forgive not only Padraic but also herself. The failure of their marriage had been a mutual defeat. But from it victory might yet be resurrected.

She turned back to the house. The door was open and through it light spilled. Padraic had waited long enough. He came toward her with firm, decisive strides that signaled his own determination.

She waited barely an instant before running to meet him.

*   *   *   *   *